What are your Superpowers?

Written by
Marget Wincent, OTR

Illustrated by
Charity Russell

Acknowledgments:

With thanks to our Creator, whose presence in my life guided me to a career and family that reflects how beautifully and wonderfully we are made.

To my parents, for their unending compassion, creativity (from baking to constructing skyscrapers), and their never-give-up attitude, I am grateful.

My journey in life is balanced by my husband, another out of the box thinker - my technology wizard, a sailor who always keeps our family moving forward, despite changes in the weather.

What are your Superpowers? is dedicated to my children, for developing my superpowers of love, humor, optimism, and fierce advocacy.

This is just a children's book, but its message comes from caring for children as a pediatric occupational therapist for over 35 years. Every family has a story, and I continue to learn and recognize the superpowers in every child. Knowing first hand that through education and awareness follows acceptance and inclusion, I want to share this important message with young children. Each page can be a springboard for discussion about a child's differences, something that makes them truly unique, viewed as their superpower!

To Charity Russell, my illustrator, for bringing my message to life through her vivid and expressive artwork.

What are your Superpowers?

Children at work, children at play,
use superpowers everyday.

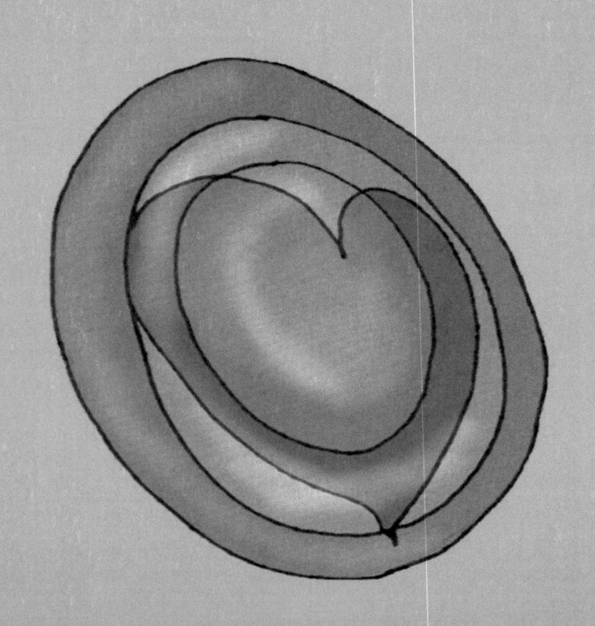

I have a four legged friend
who keeps me calm.
I'm always successful when
Mo comes along.

A B C D E F G
SERVICE
DOG

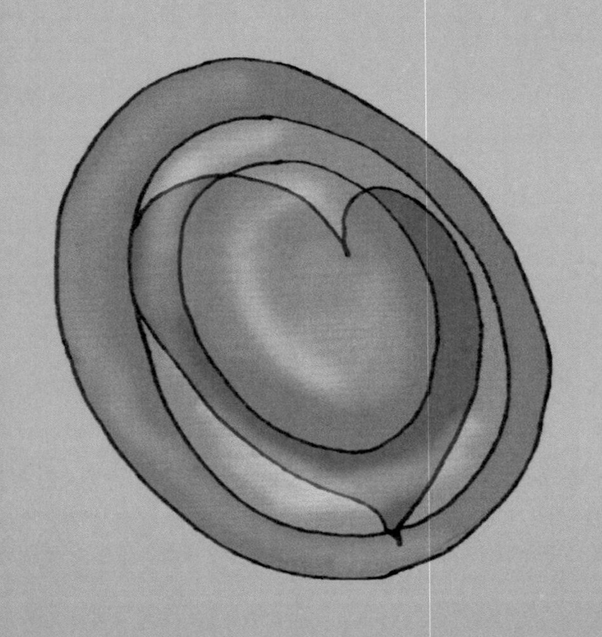

I follow pictures on schedules
because I can't ask.
Icons make sense and keep
me on task.

12
1
2
3
4
5
6
7
8
9
10
11
WAKE UP
GO TO TOILET
BREAKFAST
GET DRESSED
SCHOOL
2+2

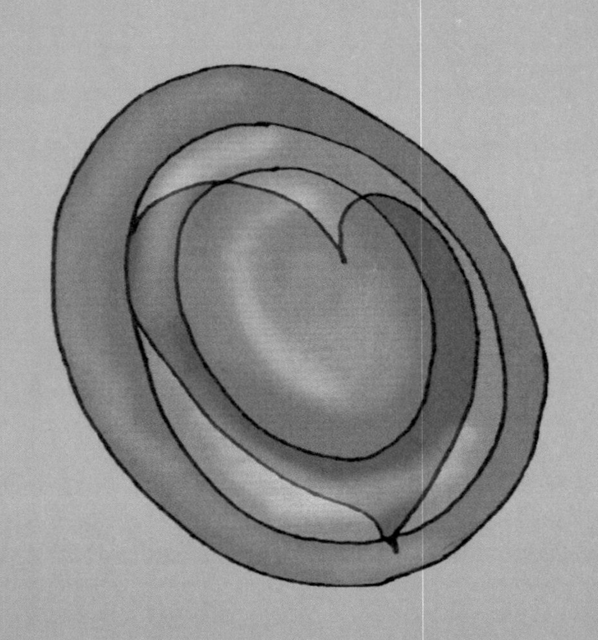

I have super speed on wheels
to zip down the hall.
My driving skills help me feel
ten feet tall!

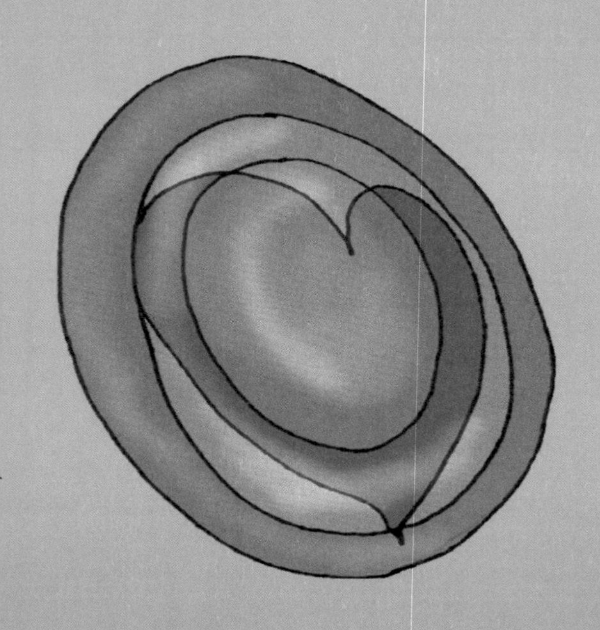

I can remember numbers
and facts that I read.
Ask me some questions
if ever in need.

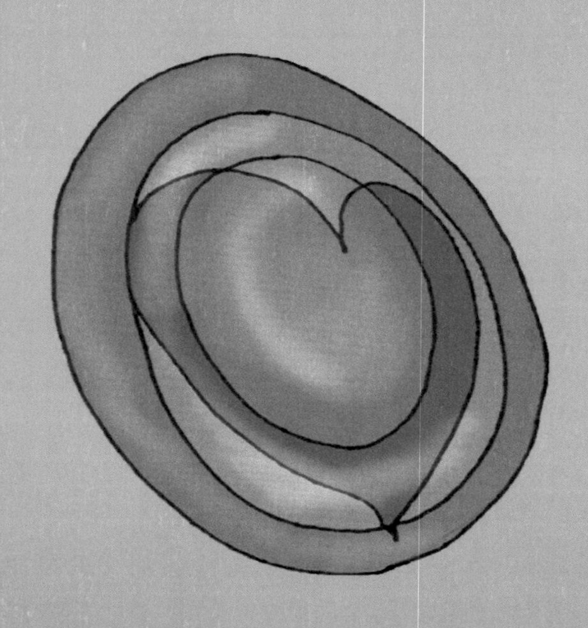

I have laser vision
at every chance.
I notice tiny details
in a single glance.

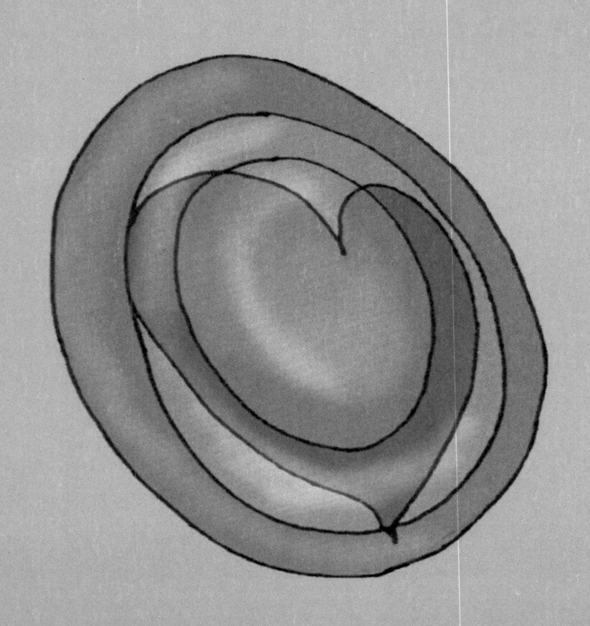

I can speak a language
without making a sound.
My hands sign the words
and never let me down.

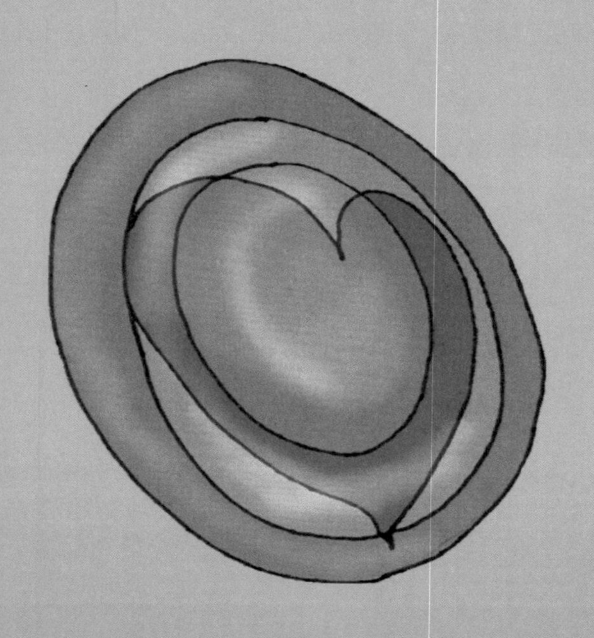

I have supersonic ears and
hear whispers all day.
Enter my space quietly
so we can play.

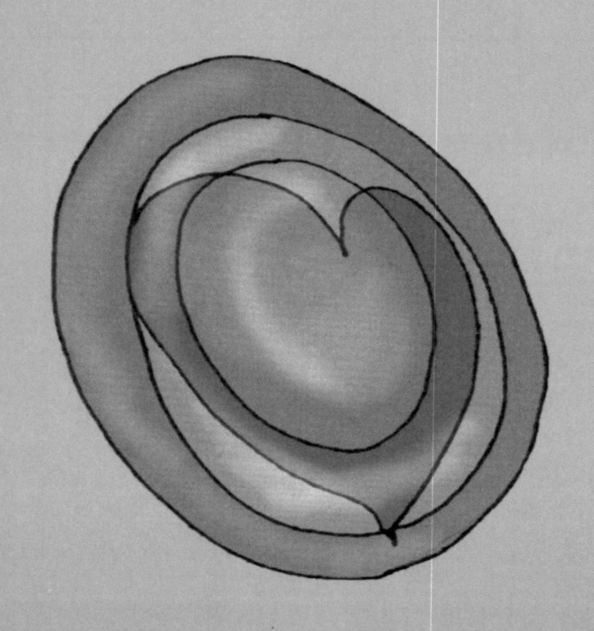

I love to sing and dance
when alone or with friends.
I always have energy
when the chorus ends.

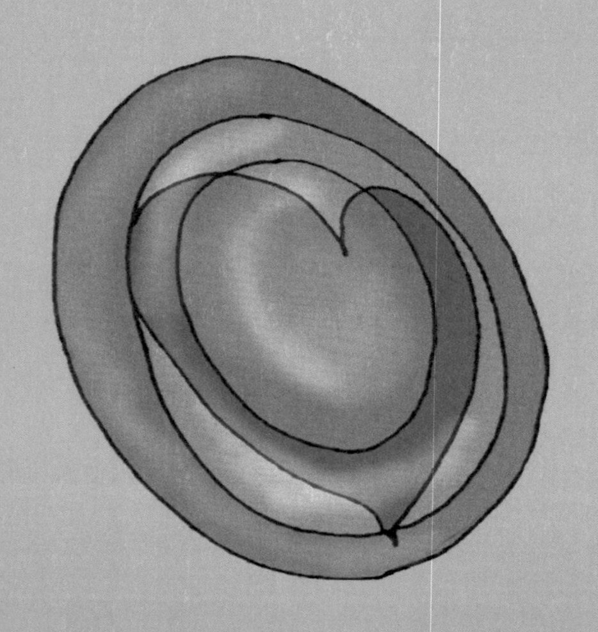

I have super taste from my
tongue to my tummy.
Let's get the blender and
make something yummy.

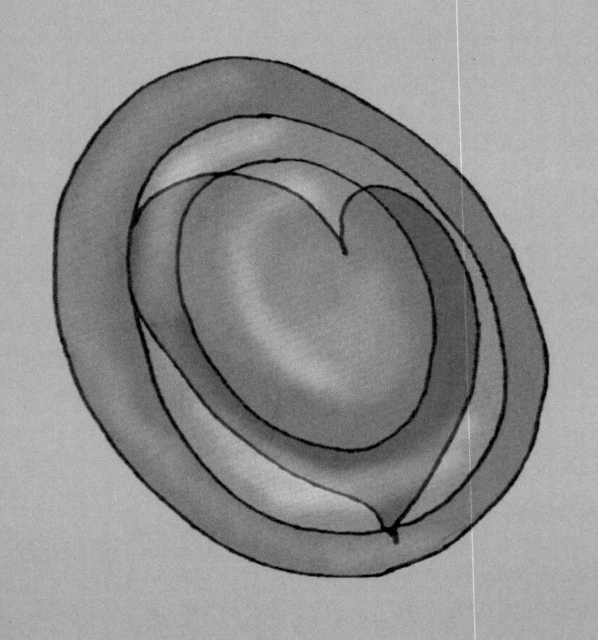

I can help tell a story
up on stage.
Acting gives me a chance
to NOT act my age.

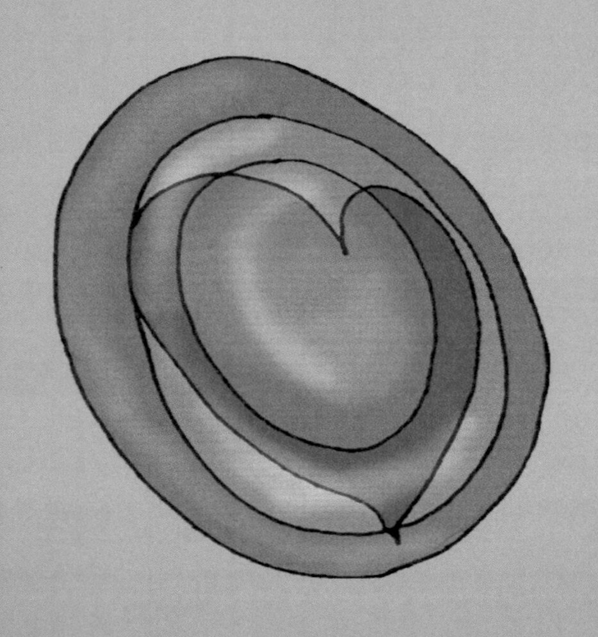

I have hands that guide
and use a cane.
I read books by touch
and that's my game.

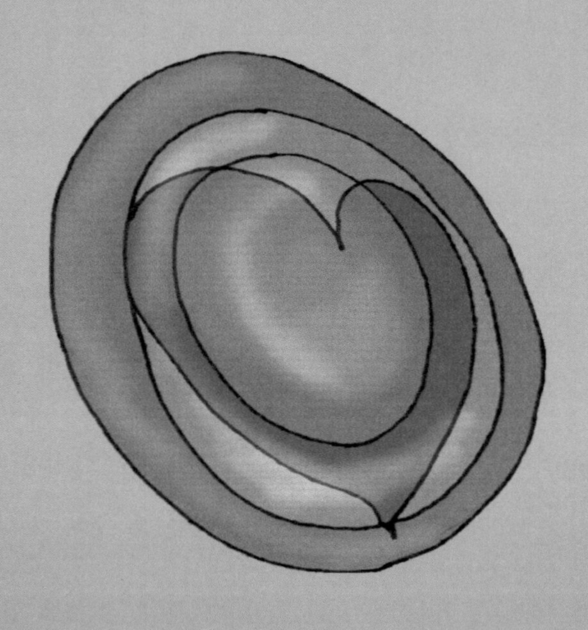

I can draw and paint
just what I see.
A growing artist
is shining in me.

STRIPE

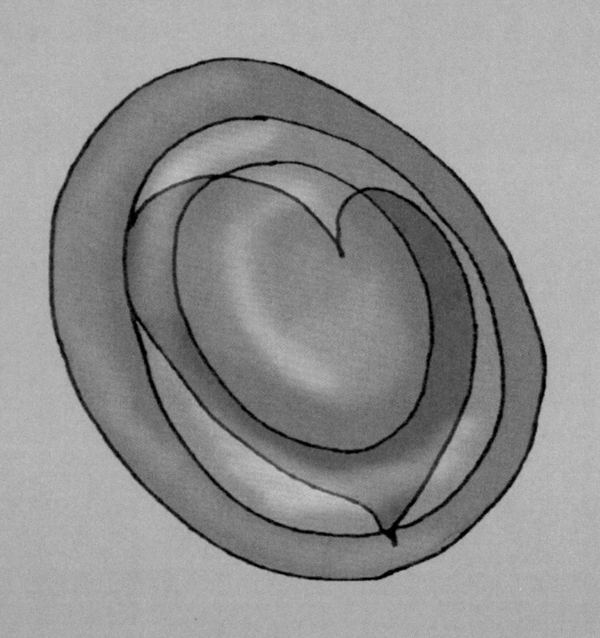

I have an emotional,
caring heart.
I can sense when your
feelings are wiggling apart.

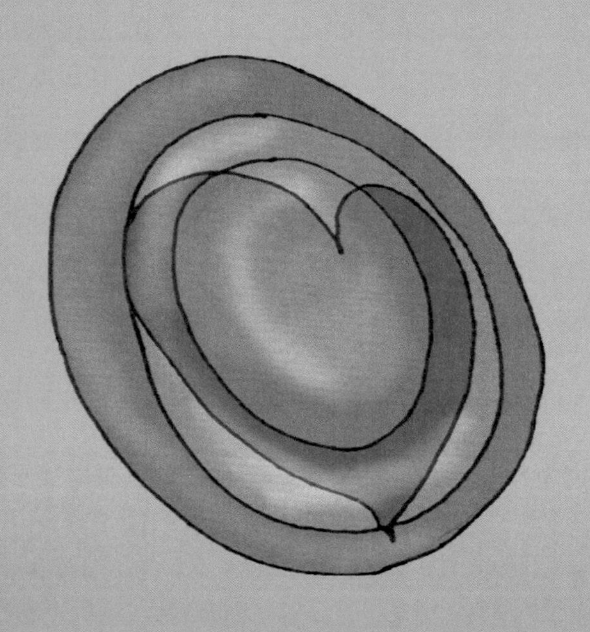

I have super balance when
trotting through trees.
Riding on Tonka
helps me feel free.

POLITE
HIPPO THERAPY ROCKS!

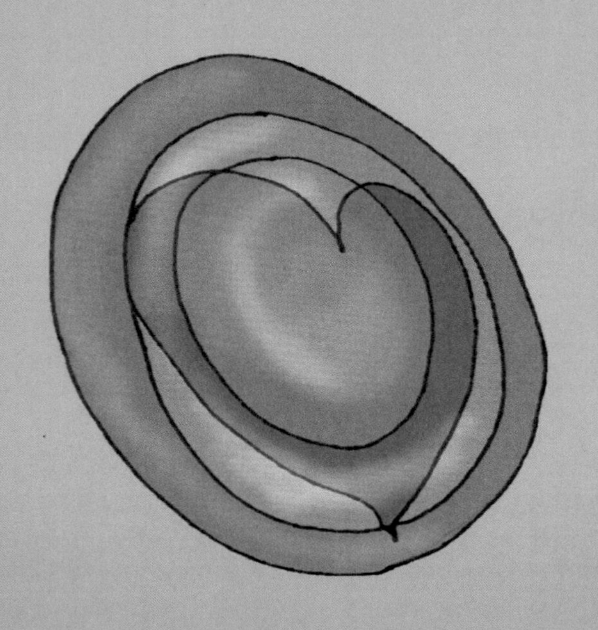

I have magic hands tossing
all types of balls.
If you need to practice,
just give me a call.

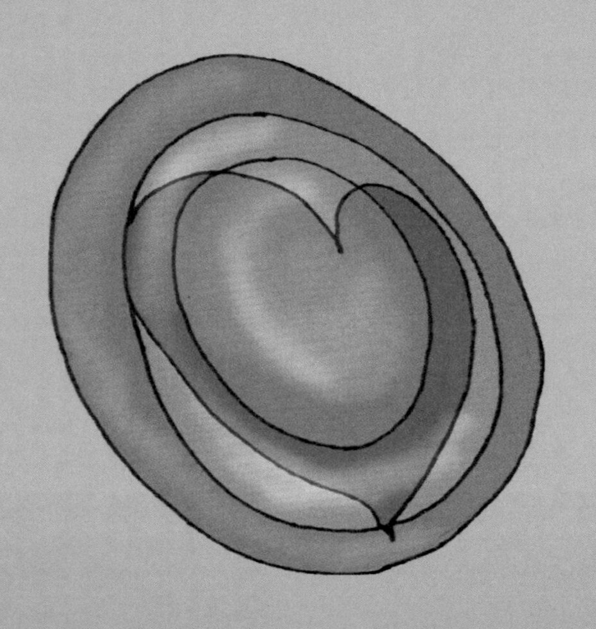

This story is ending.
Imagine all the things you do.
What are YOUR superpowers?
What makes you, YOU?

Made in the USA
Middletown, DE
14 April 2017